Autumn made her way into the kitchen.

He gestured toward his kitchen table where two mugs were laid out next to a teakettle and a plate of gingersnaps and scones. Autumn sat down across from Judah and began adding sugar and milk to it.

"You still like it sweet, huh?" Judah asked, a smile twitching at his lips.

Autumn had always had a sweet tooth. Judah used to tease her about it all the time when they'd been involved. Between milk chocolate bars and brownies, Autumn had always been craving something sweet to nibble on. "What can I say?" she asked. "Old habits die hard."

For a few moments, they both focused on their tea without any conversation.

"It's a bit strange sitting across from one another after all this time," Autumn said, eager to fill up the silence.

Judah held his mug between his hands and locked eyes with her. "I suppose so, although I always imagined you coming back home. You fit here, Autumn. I'm not sure why you ever left."

Because of you, she wanted to say.

Belle Calhoune grew up in a small town in Massachusetts. Married to her college sweetheart, she is raising two lovely daughters in Connecticut. A dog lover, she has one mini poodle and a black Lab. Writing for the Love Inspired line is a dream come true. Working at home in her pajamas is one of the best perks of the job. Belle enjoys summers in Cape Cod, traveling and reading.

Books by Belle Calhoune

Love Inspired

Serenity Peak

Her Alaskan Return
An Alaskan Christmas Promise

Home to Owl Creek

Her Secret Alaskan Family
Alaskan Christmas Redemption
An Alaskan Twin Surprise
Hiding in Alaska
Their Alaskan Past

Visit the Author Profile page at LoveInspired.com.

Her Alaskan
Return

Belle Calhoune

LOVE INSPIRED
INSPIRATIONAL ROMANCE

LOVE INSPIRED®

INSPIRATIONAL ROMANCE

Recycling programs
for this product may
not exist in your area.

ISBN-13: 978-1-335-58641-4

Her Alaskan Return

For questions and comments about the quality of this book, please contact us at CustomerService@Harlequin.com.

Love Inspired
22 Adelaide St. West, 41st Floor
Toronto, Ontario M5H 4E3, Canada
www.LoveInspired.com

Printed in U.S.A.

Fear thou not; for I am with thee: be not dismayed;
for I am thy God: I will strengthen thee; yea,
I will help thee; yea, I will uphold thee with
the right hand of my righteousness.
—*Isaiah* 41:10

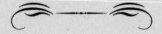

For my mother, Anne Bell.
For teaching me the important lessons
and being such a masterful storyteller.

Chapter One

A fierce Alaskan wind had kicked up over Kachemak Bay, causing large, choppy waves to churn ferociously. Judah Campbell breathed in the briny scent of the sea as he hauled in his catch of the day with a ring net. His crew celebrated with excited shouts and kudos as they spotted the bright-colored crustaceans. It was unusual for fishermen to find red Alaskan crab in February. The season for catching crab was getting shorter and shorter. Kachemak Bay was well-known for herring, salmon and halibut. This time of year certain fish were limited due to weather conditions. Finding the red Alaskan crabs made Judah feel triumphant. At this point in his life, joyful moments were rare. He intended to savor this victory.

Salmon. Halibut. He'd reeled in both over the course of the day as well as the precious crab and some clams. As an Alaskan commercial fisherman, this was his livelihood, one he deeply enjoyed. For generations, Campbells had made their living in this manner, going all the way back to his great-grandfather. Serenity Peak was only accessible by air and water, which heightened the importance of the local fishing industry. Being out on the water for so many hours allowed him to enjoy the great outdoors and to contemplate his life. Not that he had much of a life these days. Tragedy and loss had shattered him.

After his fishing boat docked back at the harbor, his crew busied themselves placing the fish on ice in boxes and making sure everything was set up for the next day. They were a well-oiled machine, having worked together for a number of years.

"Hey, guys, why don't you head out? I'll finish up," Judah called out after a few hours of solid work. He stayed behind to clean the boat and spray down the holds, knowing he didn't have anyone waiting on him at home. Gone were the days when his son would greet Judah at the door and the aroma of Mary's cooking would assault his senses the moment he stepped in the house. That knowledge caused a dull ache in the center of his chest. For all intents and purposes, he was alone.

Judah headed toward his truck in the marina parking lot and let out a sigh as he got behind the wheel and began the drive home. The rain was really coming down, and visibility was poor. He flicked on his windshield wipers and focused on the road ahead of him. Suddenly, he spotted a figure at the side of the road. Judah slowed down. A woman was standing in front of her hood being pelted by the pouring rain. He couldn't make out who it was, but it bugged him to see anyone on their own in this type of weather. Judah jerked his truck to the side of the road and parked a few feet away. As soon as he stepped down from his truck he made his way over to the vehicle, doing a double take in the process. This was one of his best friend Sean's trucks. He would know the apple red color anywhere. Had Sean loaned someone his truck?

"Hey! Is there anything I can do to help?" he asked, shouting to get the lady's attention above the sound of the torrential downpour.

The woman raised her head. Light brown eyes flecked with caramel stared back at him. Judah let out a gasp. His heart lurched clumsily in his chest. Never in a million years could he forget her eyes.

"Autumn?" he asked as shock roared through him. It had been almost eight years since he'd seen her and twelve since they'd been a couple, yet her stunning features were unmistakable. Even drenched in rain she looked wonderful. High cheekbones and warm brown skin set in a heart-shaped face tugged at him. She'd always packed quite a punch, and the years had done nothing to change that fact.

"Judah!" she said, sounding equally surprised.

"Are you all right?" He reached out and gently grasped her arm. Like the rest of her, it was soaking wet.

"Yes," she answered with a jerk of her head. "The truck wouldn't start so I figured looking under the hood might help me figure things out. This rain is ice cold." She began shivering, teeth chattering. "My cell phone died so I couldn't call a mechanic."

At the moment he was worried about Autumn freezing to death in the frigid Alaskan temps. She needed to be warmed up immediately.

"Come on and get in my truck," Judah said,

gently grasping her arm and leading her toward his ride. Once she was inside he went around to the driver's side and hopped in. He quickly dialed a local mechanic with instructions on where to find Sean's truck.

"Autumn, you need to get out of these drenched clothes ASAP. Where are you staying?" he asked.

"I'm living with Cecily until I can find my own place," she said, folding her arms around her chest.

Autumn and her younger sister had never gotten along very well, so the living arrangement was interesting in Judah's opinion. Maybe the years had softened their relationship. He sure hoped so for both their sakes.

Judah shrugged out of his warm winter parka. "Put this on and ditch that coat," he instructed, handing it to her. "Why don't I bring you to my place so you can warm up? It's only five minutes down the road. It'll take you much longer to get to your sister's house," he suggested. By that time, she would be a Popsicle. Autumn slid her arms into his jacket while he placed her sopping wet coat in a plastic bag.

"Considering I'm drenched to the bone, I'll

take you up on that," Autumn said, her voice trembling with cold.

Judah held out his hand as Autumn struggled to put her left arm in the coat. She still didn't look one hundred percent well, but once she warmed up a bit he suspected that would change. Being pelted with ice cold rain had no doubt been a shock to the system.

As she shifted her body, Judah's eyes went straight to her rounded belly. There was no mistaking the fact that she was expecting a baby.

"You're pregnant?" he asked, the words flying out of his mouth before he could rein them back in. He couldn't hide the surprise laced in his voice. Autumn was his age, thirty-nine going on forty. If they had stayed together and gotten married, he and Autumn might have had their own child by now. His chest tightened as painful memories of their breakup crashed over him. He shook them off and stuffed them down into the dark black hole he reserved for all of the agonizing moments that had gutted him over the course of his life. It did no good to dwell on past hurts. All it ever did was make him feel depressed.

He couldn't afford to let himself backslide,

not when he'd worked so hard to move past all of the moments that had threatened to break him.

Autumn saw the stunned expression on Judah's face. It wasn't the first time she'd been on the receiving end of such a perplexed look. Being almost forty and pregnant tended to raise eyebrows. With Judah, things were more complicated, due to their tangled past. Seeing her protruding belly no doubt brought him back in time to when his own wife had been pregnant with his son. Losing a child in a terrible car accident wasn't something a person ever truly got over, especially when having a family was all he'd ever wanted.

"Yes, Judah," Autumn acknowledged with a nod. "I'm pregnant."

Judah gently placed her arm into the coat and said, "Let's head to my house. I'll blast the heat to get you warmed up. How does that sound?" In response, Autumn nodded her head. She rubbed her hands together as the heat slowly began to fill the space.

Judah Campbell was still a good-looking man with a rugged physique, a strong jawline and eyes as blue as an Alaskan sky. There was a slight growth of hair on his chin and above his mouth, as if he hadn't shaved in a few days. After all these years he was still achingly handsome. But there was an air of sadness that hung over him. This man was miles apart from the one she'd once loved.

Oh, Judah. It wasn't supposed to be like this. In setting him free twelve years ago, Autumn had believed she'd been paving the path for his happily ever after. Things hadn't quite worked out the way she'd imagined.

A few seconds later Judah was driving down the road away from the fishing pier.

"I apologize if I reek of fish. After so many hours on the boat it tends to cling to me," Judah explained.

Although Autumn had detected a strong fish odor, it was the least of her concerns at the moment. Getting warm was at the top of her agenda. At this point even her bones felt cold.

"No worries. I'm just grateful for your help," she said. "I'm not sure what I would've done if you hadn't driven by."

"Happy to be there." Judah turned toward her. "What were you doing at the pier?"

She wrinkled her nose. Going out on the pier in bad weather hadn't been her most brilliant move. "There was a sea lion in the water that I wanted to take a picture of so I walked out on to the pier. I should have turned back when I realized it was starting to storm. Long story short, when I headed back to Sean's truck it wouldn't start." She shivered. "Of all the times for my phone to die on me."

"You've got to make sure it's charged, Autumn. What if you have an emergency with the baby?" he asked.

She hated to admit it, but Judah was right. It had been irresponsible of her to place herself in this position. Feeling humbled, Autumn didn't have the heart to respond.

"I know from what Sean told me that you're a writer in New York City," Judah said. He was clearly trying to fill the silence with conversation.

She always forgot that her brother Sean and Judah were still such good friends. From what she'd heard, Judah didn't have much to do with most of the townsfolk in Serenity Peak. She didn't know the whole story, but it was tied up in the loss of his wife and son.

"Yes. I love being a writer. It's a gift to be able to do something you enjoy, much like yourself." Judah had always yearned to be a commercial fisherman, following in his father's footsteps. He'd always said that the ocean brought out the best in him. She prayed that was still true.

Autumn couldn't get over the shock of coming face-to-face with her first love in such dramatic circumstances. According to Sean, Judah had become a bit of a hermit over the past few years, so she truly hadn't expected to see him so soon. "I'm grateful you were nearby to help me. I don't want to think about how long I might have been out there in the rain if you hadn't rescued me."

"I'm glad I was there too. That's the true beauty of a community, banding together to help one another. Or that's the way it should be." A tremor jumped along his jawline. His words sounded sarcastic to Autumn's ears. She had a feeling he was referencing something personal.

Judah began to navigate the truck onto the main road. Autumn drank in the sights of Serenity Peak that she hadn't seen in years. The craggy facade of the Serenity Mountains. A small seaplane as it dipped down across Kachemak Bay. A bald eagle soaring gracefully in the sky.

"I had no idea you were back in Serenity Peak. When did you come home?" Judah asked.

Her teeth began to chatter. She was still chilled to the bone. "J-just yesterday, Judah. I flew in from Fairbanks."

"Any reason you came back? I thought you were eager to get away from small towns and Alaska."

She cringed. Judah was bringing up one of their last face-to-face meetings. At the time, Autumn had been young and desperate to sever all ties with Judah and her small town. She'd said so many things she really hadn't meant to cover up her broken heart. Breaking up with him had been her misguided attempt to make sure Judah was able to live out his dream of having children. She had sacrificed her own happiness so he could become a father one day.

"That was a lifetime ago. So much has changed since then," she acknowledged.

"I won't argue with you on that point," Judah conceded, making a face.

"I'm already five months along with my pregnancy. I've given it a lot of thought and I want to raise my child here in Serenity Peak where I grew up. I'm thinking of this as a permanent move." Autumn's childhood had been wonderful. She and her three siblings had been well-loved by their parents. Alaska had been a great stomping ground for their adventures. She wanted no less for her little one. "I'll be able to work remotely while being employed as a writer."

Judah said, "Your plan makes sense. There's no better place to live than Alaska." A quick glance in his direction showed a shuttered expression. He seemed incredibly guarded, so much more so than when they'd been head over heels in love with one another. It hadn't escaped her notice that Judah hadn't congratulated her for being pregnant. What did she expect? He'd lost so very much in his own life. Why should he be happy for her?

"I was sorry to hear about your wife. And your son," Autumn said. She knew that she was dodging landmines in bringing up Judah's family tragedy, but she couldn't ignore it. Losing his wife, Mary, and their son so horrifically must have been devastating for Judah. Ever since then, according to Sean, Judah had been a loner, cutting himself off from the residents of Serenity Peak. All she knew from Sean was that someone had started a cruel rumor that Mary had been on pills before the crash. Autumn didn't know much more than that tidbit. It had been enough to alienate Judah from the townsfolk in Serenity Peak.

Judah clenched his jaw. "Thanks," he said tersely. "Life isn't always fair."

An awkward silence filled the air until Judah turned down a road lined by snow-covered Sitka trees. He pulled into a driveway leading to a modest, log cabin style home. Autumn knew immediately that this was a far cry from the home Judah had grown up in and had inherited from his dad. She wasn't surprised he had renovated the place to meet current trends. The Campbell family's house had been old-fashioned and in need of updates. Regardless of that detail, the home had always been full of love.

After putting his truck in Park, Judah quickly made his way to the passenger side and helped her down. He was still a gentleman, she realized. These same gestures had been one of the reasons she'd fallen so fast and hard for him. He had made her feel incredibly safe and well loved.

As they walked along the snowy path toward his house, Autumn spotted two cedar Adirondack chairs sitting on his front porch. She knew without asking that they were Abel Drummond's creations. Among other things, he was an accomplished woodworker. His craftsmanship had always been impeccable.

Judah opened up the door and ushered her inside from the cold. Although she'd warmed up in the truck, her wet clothes still felt uncomfortable. As it was, she didn't want to drip on his gleaming hardwood floors. She was beginning to feel like an imposition.

The sound of nails clicking on the hardwood floors heralded the arrival of a medium-sized Irish setter who flew to Judah's side. "Hey, Delilah," he said, bending over and lavishing the dog with attention. "Did you miss me, girl?" Delilah answered by licking the side of Judah's jaw.

"She's a beauty," Autumn said, admiring the glossy sheen of Delilah's coat. She hoped to get a dog of her own when her child was a bit older.

"She is. I have a dog walker who comes to the house a few times a day when I'm working so she's not cooped up. Delilah loves the outdoors."

The canine began curiously sniffing Autumn, who patted her on the head in return.

"Okay, that's enough girl," he said, gently pushing the Irish setter. He swung his gaze to Autumn. "Why don't you take a hot shower in the guest bedroom bathroom? While you're in there I'll put some clothes on the bed for you. I'm going to take one myself to wash my day at sea off. Then I can make us some hot tea. Sound good?"

"Yes, it does," she said, feeling comforted by the idea of a shower and some soothing tea. Autumn followed after Judah as he led her down the hall.

"Everything you need will be in the bathroom closet. I'll see you in a bit," Judah said with a nod.

Autumn went into the bathroom, shutting the door behind her. She peeled off her wet clothes and hopped into the shower. She shut her eyes as the warm water cascaded over her body. She took her time warming up before toweling off and heading into the bedroom. A stack of clothes awaited her—a hunter green sweatshirt, thick socks, a pair of sweats.

They were men's clothing so Autumn didn't have to deal with the discomfort of wearing his deceased wife's apparel. Even though the items were big on her, Autumn felt wonderful being in dry clothes. When she made her way into the kitchen, Judah took her wet clothes and placed them in the dryer. He gestured toward his kitchen table where two mugs were laid out next to a tea kettle and a plate of ginger snaps and scones. Autumn sat down across from Judah and began adding sugar and milk to it.

"You still like it sweet, huh?" Judah asked, a smile twitching at his lips.

Autumn had always had a sweet tooth. Judah used to tease her about it all the time when they'd been involved. Between milk chocolate bars and brownies, Autumn had always been craving something sweet to nibble on. "What can I say?" she asked. "Old habits die hard."

For a few moments they both focused on their tea without any conversation.

"It's a bit strange sitting across from one another after all this time," Autumn said, eager to fill up the silence.

Judah held his mug between his hands and locked eyes with her. "I suppose so, although I always imagined you coming back home. You fit here, Autumn. I'm not sure why you ever left."

Because of you, she wanted to say. *And Mary.* A few months after her breakup with Judah he'd started dating Mary. Seeing them together had nearly ripped her heart out. She had almost run back to Judah and begged him to take her back. Leaving had been her only sensible option. How could she have stuck around and watched Judah fall in love with another woman? To marry Mary and build a family with her? It would have cut sharper than a knife. Being on the East Coast had allowed her to build a life without having to watch Judah live out his dreams with someone else. But she couldn't say any of those things because Judah had no idea of the huge secret she'd kept from him for all of these years. She would have given anything to carry his child and make a life with him.

Her doctor had informed her that due to severe endometriosis she would never be able to conceive a child. As she struggled to accept the devastating news, Autumn had decided to end things so Judah could move on and have the family of his dreams. Only she hadn't told him about her inability to bear future children. Knowing Judah, he would have sacrificed his wishes for a family to be with her. And she would never have forgiven herself. And he would have grown to resent her.

God worked in mysterious ways. Finally, so many years after her shocking diagnosis, Autumn was pregnant. She'd long since given up on hoping for a child of her very own, so this was truly a gift from above. Even though her marriage to Jay had ended in divorce due to his infidelity, she was grateful for this baby. A dream come to fruition.

Thank you for this blessing, Lord.

"Well, I'm home now," she said, pushing away the old memories, choosing instead to focus on the here and now. It was all in the past. With a baby on the way, Autumn's future was clear. She would make her child her number one priority. Part of doing so was ensuring that she still had a career in journalism. Being able to work remotely from Serenity Peak was an incredible blessing. If she had to travel from time to time to investigate leads, Autumn would make that work as well. Having family nearby would be crucial to her plans.

"You've completely renovated the place. I wouldn't even recognize it." Back in the day she'd sat at the Campbells' dinner table countless times and enjoyed Mama Campbell's down-home cooking. The home still had a rustic vibe, but she could no longer view it as old-fashioned. He'd brought it into the twenty-first century.

"Yeah," he acknowledged with a bob of his head. "It was Mary's idea. She thought it would breathe new life into the place."

Autumn didn't know what to say. It was

terribly sad that Mary was no longer around to enjoy seeing her plans come to pass. "Well, she did a beautiful job. It's lovely." She picked up another scone and bit into it, enjoying the flavorful berry taste as it landed on her tongue.

"Is your husband arriving soon?" Judah pressed, his eyes brimming with curiosity.

She sucked in a fortifying breath before answering. "I'm not married anymore. The divorce papers were already in progress when I found out that I was expecting." She placed her hand on her belly, noticing how Judah's gaze landed on her abdomen before quickly glancing away.

"And you didn't want to try and save the marriage?" he asked, his eyes widening.

Autumn took a deep breath before responding. How many times had she been asked this question by well-meaning friends back in New York? Too many to count if memory served her correctly. Explaining was never easy.

"It was beyond salvaging. We had too many lifestyle differences to make it work." She sensed from the look etched on Judah's face that he wanted her to elaborate. "He's a musician who tours around the country a lot.

And when he's not touring he does gigs that don't end until the wee hours of the morning. The two of us barely saw each other and then he had an affair with one of his backup singers that went on for months," she admitted. This was her truth and even though she feared being judged for the hard choices she'd made, Autumn wanted to be honest. It had taken her a long time to get past feeling ashamed that she hadn't lived out her happily ever after. She bit her lip. "We tried to make things work for a very long time, but all we did was argue. Neither one of us wanted to live that way."

"And the baby?" he asked, his voice sounding gruff. "It'll be tough being a father all the way from New York City, won't it?"

"The doors will always be open for him to be involved in his child's life. I would never take that away from him. On my end I'll do everything possible to make sure he can serve that role if he wants to," Autumn said. And she meant it. "To be honest, having this baby is a blessing. If I end up doing it all by myself, I'll embrace my role as mother with open arms."

She didn't want to get into it with Judah, but Autumn wasn't sure her ex-husband saw a place in his life for a child. That was one of the most painful parts of her marriage. She'd been only in her early twenties when told she could never bear a child. She'd carried that pain around with her for a very long time. Her infertility had never mattered to Jay, but in hindsight, she now knew it had been his preference to be a permanently childless couple. His reaction to her pregnancy news had been a mixture of disappointment and anger. He'd expressed to her that he had never wanted a child and couldn't imagine his life as a father. That had spoken volumes. She'd known at that point that their lives were on different paths and that the decision to file for divorce had been the right one. Finding out about his affair had truly shattered their marriage.

God offered up blessings when you least expected it. This baby was an absolute gift from above. She would make motherhood her main priority. Autumn had no intention of squandering this chance.

Coming home to Alaska wasn't as simple as she'd conveyed to Judah. She hadn't told him everything, although she knew he would find out soon enough. Gossip flew around Serenity Peak like high-flying kites. Autumn now worked for the *Alaska Tribune*. She'd been hired to write about the local Alaskan community, starting with an article about the commercial fishing industry in the Kenai Peninsula. Her initial research had uncovered the possibility that there was a federal investigation being launched into acts of fraud being committed by commercial fisherman, allegations that could lead straight back to Judah.

Chapter Two

Once Autumn's clothes finished drying, Judah waited in the kitchen as she changed back into her attire. He was still trying to wrap his head around the events of the past few hours. Not only was Autumn back in Serenity Peak, but she was pregnant and he'd rescued her from a torrential downpour after her car broke down. Although they'd parted ways twelve years ago, the memories of their love story were still sharp in his mind. He and Autumn had been together for a period of seven years. They had started dating each other when they were twenty.

Judah had wanted her to be his girlfriend since they were teenagers, but out of respect for Sean, he'd steered clear of her. Autumn had been the one to pursue him when they grew older, and with Sean's approval, they had become a couple.

At one point in time Judah had believed they would grow old together. He had even made plans to restore his mother's engagement ring and propose to Autumn. Judah had only waited to make sure Fishful Thinking got off the ground and he could make a comfortable living for them. He let out a brittle laugh. Those dreams had crashed and burned. To this day he wasn't all that certain why Autumn ended things between them, but for Judah it had been heart-wrenching.

A heads-up that Autumn had returned would have been nice. He stuffed down a burst of irritation that Sean hadn't told him she was coming home to Serenity Peak. He was his best friend—one of his only buddies in Serenity Peak. After the accident and the disgusting rumors about Mary, Judah had cut his ties with almost everyone in town. Every now and again Sean gave him little breadcrumbs about Autumn's life. A part of him had always felt disloyal to Mary for craving such tidbits about his ex-girlfriend. It wasn't that he'd carried a torch for her, but he had always been curious about her life away from Alaska.

Seeing her rounded belly had caused a groundswell of grief to rise up inside of him, not only for the dreams he'd once harbored for the two of them but for his son, Zane. Sometimes it all hit him at the most unexpected times—a feeling of loss as deep as the ocean. Even as a kid it had been Judah's desire to have a house full of children he could raise and shower with love. Those hopes had been snuffed out by events outside of his control. He'd held his tongue while talking to Autumn about her ex-husband. What kind of man, he wondered, wouldn't want to be a part of his child's life? It was unfathomable.

His cell phone rang, and he saw Brody Locke's name pop up on his caller ID. Brody was a member of Judah's crew. He'd shown himself to be loyal and hardworking over the past five years. He was also someone Judah knew he could trust implicitly.

"Hey, boss," Brody said. "I wanted to discuss something with you if you have a few minutes."

"Hi, Brody. Is it all right if I circle back to you? It's not a good time for me to talk." A long pause ensued with no response from Brody.

"Is everything okay?" Judah asked after a few beats of silence.

Brody let out a ragged sigh. "I got some intel from a friend in Homer. A lot of wild rumors are circulating that you might want to hear."

Judah clenched his teeth. Gossip had been circulating for weeks about a federal investigation into reporting irregularities. Although he had tried to discount the rumors as nonsense, the chatter was getting too loud to ignore. It was hitting way too close to home. This wasn't the first time word had gotten back to him either. According to the rumor mill, Fishful Thinking seemed to be in the crosshairs, which made absolutely no sense. Judah would never fail to report his catch or doctor his logbooks. He was an ethical fisherman who couldn't live with himself if he broke the rules for profit. He knew some fishermen caught more fish than was legally allowed, deliberately mislabeled fish or ventured into areas that were off limits to secure certain fish, but he wasn't one of them. He made his living honestly.

"Let's grab some coffee outside of work," Judah suggested. "Thanks for looking out for me, Brody. I'll talk to you later." His chest swelled at the loyalty Brody exhibited.

The sound of light footsteps alerted him to

Autumn's approach. As she walked over the threshold to the kitchen, Judah sucked in a steadying breath at the sight of her. The ensuing years had only served to heighten her beauty. Tall and lean, in another life Autumn could have been a model gracing the covers of magazines or an Olympic athlete. But those endeavors had never appealed to her. She had always been interested in writing and the arts.

"I feel almost back to normal. And no longer like a drowned rat," Autumn said, smiling. "Judah, I can't thank you enough for being so gracious."

"You don't have to thank me. I would have done it for anyone." He saw Autumn flinch in response to his comment. *Why had he spoken so roughly?* Perhaps it was tied up in their past relationship and the way things had ended between them. Losing Autumn had truly crushed Judah. She had abruptly broken things off with him and he wasn't even certain what had gone wrong. One day she'd been in love with him and in the next, she'd wanted to end things. Judah had always felt that Autumn had given up on their relationship while he'd fought to keep them together. He couldn't help but wonder if she was doing the same thing with her husband.

"I should get out of your way," Autumn said. "Would you mind dropping me off at my sister's now? Hopefully I'll get word tomorrow about Sean's truck."

"Sure thing," he said. "Let me grab our coats. Come on, Delilah. You can come for the ride." Delilah began wagging her tail before running over to the front door to wait for them.

Judah brought Autumn the long olive green parka and held it out for her to slip her arms through. In the process his fingers brushed across her arm, causing a frisson of awareness to wash over him. It was muscle memory, he figured. His heart had belonged to her for so many years. He wasn't in love with her anymore, but it had taken him such a long time to get Autumn out of his heart and mind. She had been his entire world. To this day little pieces of her were imprinted on his heart.

Her face was impassive, as if she had no clue how she still affected him. *Good*, he thought. Judah didn't want Autumn to have that power over him. The way she had in their relationship when he would have grabbed the stars from the sky if she'd asked him.

Why was he dredging up the past? Doing

so made him feel disloyal to his deceased wife. Mary had once accused him of using her as a rebound romance to get over Autumn. A part of him knew it was true, yet he'd never admitted it. He'd loved his wife, but what they'd shared hadn't been moonlight and roses. A flicker of memory flashed into his mind—Autumn with the wind blowing through her hair as she stood on the deck of Fishful Thinking as he navigated the boat across the bay. The rich sound of her laughter had made his soul soar.

Stop! That was a lifetime ago. He forced himself back to the present. Judah needed to get as far away as possible from Autumn. He couldn't drop her off at her sister's house fast enough. Moving forward was his main objective in life.

Getting caught up in his past with Autumn wasn't a good idea. Judah didn't think he would survive it a second time around.

Once again, Judah came forward to help her step up into his truck. Autumn had to admit she'd missed being in the presence of a gentleman who opened doors and held out her chair. At his core, Judah was a caretaker, Autumn realized. He'd always been invested in the welfare of others. She imagined he'd been that way with his family.

Some instinct told her that Judah didn't have guests often, which made his gesture to invite her over even more meaningful. Strangely enough, Autumn hadn't spotted a single photograph of Mary and their son. Not one. Matter of fact, Autumn hadn't seen any pictures at all on display. It was a bit odd considering how much family had always meant to him. Growing up in this very same house there had always been photos on every mantle and wall.

Perhaps he didn't want to be reminded of everything he'd lost. She felt a pang in her heart. She hated the fact that he'd endured so much. For a man like Judah who'd only ever wanted a family of his own, his current situation was devastating.

"The town feels different," Autumn noted as they drove past the town square and Fifth Street where most of the stores were located. She spotted several new shops—a charming bookstore–coffee shop, a lovely jewelry shop, as well as an artist's studio. Serenity Peak had always been a haven for creative people, so it was only fitting to see these specialty stores in existence.

"When was the last time you were here?" Judah asked. "Serenity Peak isn't the same place we grew up in."

"About three years ago. I came home for Skye's wedding." She let out a sigh. "Or should I say the wedding that wasn't. It was sad to see all of her hopes and dreams crushed." Perhaps she related to the young woman due to her own disappointments in her twenties. Heartache wasn't easy to live through. Frankly, she wasn't sure how she'd survived it.

Skye Drummond was the daughter of one of the founding families of Serenity Peak. They ran Sugar Works, a birch syrup company that sold all over the world. She was young and a bit on the wild side. Growing up, her older sister, Violet, had been Autumn's best friend. It wasn't any of her business, but Tyler Flint had been right to pull the plug on their wedding. Skye hadn't been ready to settle down. Not by a long shot. However, ditching someone so close to the wedding day was cruel. Autumn hated how Skye had been treated.

He nodded. "You're right," he acknowledged. "A lot has changed. We've had an influx of folks wanting to relocate here due to our healthy fishing industry and the hot springs. Not to mention Sugar Works is still a household name in Alaska. A lot of jobs have opened up there."

"Serenity Peak has always been popular with tourists looking for a tranquil Alaskan experience," she said. "No better town in the state to offer calm and serenity."

"I wouldn't describe this town that way, but then again, I'm an outsider these days. From time to time I run excursions on my boat for tourists, but other than that I keep away from the goings-on in town." Judah sounded so matter of fact, as if he couldn't care less about their hometown or the residents. His indifference was unsettling. It was as if he had retreated so far inside himself that the Judah she'd once known had disappeared.

"That's hard to picture." Although she knew that Judah harbored anger toward town residents, it was still hard to wrap her head around it. At the time of Judah's loss Autumn hadn't wanted to know all of the details about the town gossip. Being told by Sean that Judah was out of sorts and grieving had been painful to hear. Letting go of him all those years ago had been so he could live his best life. She'd never imagined he would lose so much. His world had collapsed in an instant.

A tight feeling spread across her chest just thinking about it.

"Your family was always a big part of Serenity Peak. Town mayors. Shop owners. Teachers. The commercial fishing community. Has that changed as well?" she asked, filled with curiosity about the current state of affairs.

Judah shrugged. "I can only speak for myself. The fishing community is my only connection to this town. My nephew Ryan is now a member of law enforcement so I suppose the Campbells are still in the thick of things. He's grown up to be a good man."

Autumn could hear the pride ringing out in Judah's voice. Ryan had been a child the last time she'd seen him, serving as a reminder of how many years stood between her and this town. She probably wouldn't even recognize him if she passed him on the street. Autumn didn't dare ask about Judah's brother, Leif. She knew they were estranged, but she didn't know the particulars. Yet another tremendous loss for Judah. He and Leif had always been joined at the hip.

"At least the economy is healthy. I've been hearing lots of stories about Alaskan towns that are struggling with their ability to keep their shops open and haul in plentiful amounts of fish. It's rough out there."

"My operation has been blessed, but the Alaskan fishing industry as a whole has been hit with fish shortages, which ultimately affects the bottom line." He cast a quick glance in her direction. "You seem pretty knowledgeable about Alaskan commercial fishing. Since when does it interest you?" he asked, his brows furrowed.

"Sean must've mentioned it in our conversations," Autumn answered. "He's got a vested interest in making sure the local fish supply is solid."

Her brother owned one of the most popular restaurants in Serenity Peak called Northern Lights. Seafood dishes were some of the establishment's most popular fare. Both of her parents worked there along with Cecily and other members of her large family. Judah had a share in the business but wasn't there often according to Sean. His main role was arranging for fresh fish deliveries several times a week.

Autumn felt a bit guilty. All of this information she'd spouted about the commercial fishing business was material she'd researched in order to write her article. Was it wrong to withhold this information from Judah? It was awkward since his fishing operation was potentially under scrutiny. She'd always been professional as a journalist. Maintaining her standards in difficult circumstances was something she was proud of. Bending the rules wasn't her style. Not even for Judah and what they'd once meant to each other.

As they drove down the heavily forested mountain road, Autumn took a moment to soak in her surroundings. Wide-open spaces. Gorgeous trees blanketed in snow. A moose crossing sign—not exactly something you saw in New York City. This is what she had missed most about Serenity Peak. It offered a tranquility she'd never quite been able to find anywhere else. Judah put the brakes on as a graceful deer darted into the road. He glanced over at her. "Once you see one—"

"There's bound to be more," Autumn said, finishing his sentence. It was a Serenity Peak saying, one she'd heard hundreds of times ever since she was a child. Seconds later three more deer, including a foal, ambled across the road. Autumn let out a chuckle. The sight of the deer family made her feel all warm and fuzzy inside. She'd missed out on moments like this one. Never again would she take them for granted.

As soon as Judah pulled up in front of Cecily's modest ranch-style home, the front door flew open as if her sister had been expecting them. Within moments, Cecily came rushing toward the truck.

She seemed to catch Judah off guard by giving him a bear hug as soon as he stepped out of the truck. All Autumn could do was watch as Judah squirmed. Her ex wasn't the most demonstrative person so she sensed his slight discomfort. Thankfully, Judah and Cecily were old friends. From the very first time Sean had brought him home the entire Hines family had fallen in love with him.

"Hey, Judah," Cecily said. "It's been ages since I've seen you. How are you doing?"

"Hi, Cici," Judah said, greeting her by her childhood nickname. "I can't complain. I've been keeping busy out on the bay. Even caught some red crabs. Still your favorite?"

"I could eat crab every day of the week," her sister replied. Her natural rapport with Judah made Autumn wish she could relax around him as Cecily did.

"Well, I'm going to get going. Gotta head out early tomorrow morning," Judah explained.

"Don't be a stranger, Judah," Cecily said, placing her hand on Judah's arm. "I've been making that mixed berry pie you used to love so much for the customers at Northern Lights. Just say the word and I'll save you some slices." With a wave, Cecily walked back toward the house.

Autumn envied their congenial relationship. Things felt so strained between her and Judah. Before they'd ever fallen in love, she and Judah had been the best of friends.

"Thanks again for the save, Judah," Autumn said. "I have no idea what would have happened if you weren't there." She owed Judah big-time.

"I'm glad I was at the pier at that exact moment in time," he said with a slight smile. For the first time since she'd seen him at the wharf he resembled the old Judah, the one who'd been full of light and laughter. With a nod he stepped up into his vehicle and got behind the wheel before roaring off.

After Autumn stepped inside the house she walked straight toward the kitchen in search of Cecily.

"What were you doing with Judah?" Cecily asked, wiggling her eyebrows as she turned toward her. Her sister had a huge smirk on her face.

Autumn counted to ten in her head. Suddenly it felt like they were back in high school all over again with Cecily being all in her business. Maybe she should have stayed with Sean and his family, but she had declined her brother's invitation. Having her as a houseguest would have overcrowded his modest sized home. As a result, she now had to deal with her sister.

"I'm not sure why it matters, but Sean's truck broke down and I was looking under the hood in the downpour. Judah drove by and spotted me right when I needed help." Just saying the words out loud sounded surreal. Cecily didn't need to know he'd taken her back to his place. If she did tell her sister the whole story, the news would be spread all around Serenity Peak in the blink of an eye. The entire town would be whispering about her and Judah reuniting at the harbor.

Her sister let out a tutting sound. "It didn't take you guys long."

Autumn folded her arms across her chest. "What is that supposed to mean?"

Cecily shrugged. "I knew you and Judah would be drawn to one another like magnets."

"It wasn't anything like that," she said with a shake of her head. "You know Judah. It would be impossible for him to keep driving once he spotted someone in need. I'm five months pregnant, and I haven't laid eyes on Judah in years. I can't believe you think I'm chasing after him."

"I wasn't suggesting anything of the sort!" Cecily huffed, placing her hands on her hips. "It's called chemistry. You and Judah have always had it. I was simply saying that I wasn't surprised to see the two of you together. Honestly, I never understood why the two of you broke up in the first place."

Autumn twisted her mouth. "That's old news. Sometimes things just don't work out. I don't understand why you're dredging up the past when we both moved on ages ago."

Her sister quirked her mouth. "I've always had the feeling that there was more to the story, but we've never been close as sisters, so I understand why you didn't confide in me. But I couldn't help but notice that after Judah started seeing Mary you moved away from Serenity Peak and created a new life for yourself. With a husband I might add. And now you're having the baby of your dreams as a single woman. You haven't lived here for over a decade. Why did you come back to Serenity Peak?"

The question gave Autumn pause. Why had she come back home after all this time? From the moment her doctor had confirmed Autumn's pregnancy she'd known that Serenity Peak would be her baby's home. There was no other place in the world Autumn would consider. Cecily was making her question her actions. Hadn't this been the right decision? Wasn't she wanted in her hometown? Now, with a few probing questions from Cecily, she was full of indecision.

Why did it rattle her so much to have come face-to-face with Judah? She'd fallen out of love with him a long time ago, but she couldn't pretend as if they didn't share a connection. She'd known him all her life. Seeing him again truly felt like a homecoming. If she had trusted him more back then, maybe she would have told him the truth about her infertility diagnosis. At the time she had been ashamed and worried that he might stop loving her. Sometimes it nagged at her. What might have been if she'd simply been honest. She had single-handedly destroyed their relationship.

Instead of answering Cecily, Autumn headed to the spare guest room to escape her sister's needling and lie down. Why had she accepted Cecily's offer to stay at her house? They had been at odds for most of their lives so she shouldn't be surprised that they were butting heads. Autumn placed a hand on her stomach and lightly rubbed it. She didn't need any additional stress in her life. At five months along, she was firmly established in her pregnancy, yet she also knew her age made this pregnancy high risk.

Please, Lord. Protect this precious life. Let me bring this child safely into the world with no complications.

Being back in Serenity Peak was going to be tricky with her pregnancy, finding a place of her own to live and investigating the piece she was researching on the local fishing industry. She would need to go out into the field to interview people in order to flesh out her article and talk to the authorities. Maybe even make some day trips to Homer and Fairbanks. She'd been hired by the *Tribune* as a full-time staffer and there were several other pieces she'd received the green light to write.

Autumn prayed nothing would lead back to Judah or his company despite the rumors swirling around about his operation. So far all it amounted to was speculation and gossip. In a small town like Serenity Peak, folks loved to run their mouths.

Judah had lost enough in his life over the years. Autumn didn't want to be the reason his life was turned upside down all over again.

Chapter Three

Bright and early the next morning, Autumn headed over to the doctor's office for a pre-natal checkup. Despite reassurances from her doctor in New York, she continued to worry about something going wrong with her pregnancy. Thankfully, this appointment had been set up for her weeks ago to allay her fears. It was difficult to feel secure in carrying a baby at this point in her life. Autumn knew she would only be able to fully relax once her baby was safely delivered and given a clean bill of health. She was counting the days until she could hold the baby in her arms.

Dr. Poppy Matthews was a striking young woman with stunning African braids, a lovely mahogany complexion and a warm personal-ity. She immediately put Autumn at ease by asking her to call her Poppy rather than the more formal Dr. Matthews.

"Thanks for having your doctor send your file to me, Autumn," Poppy said. "I was able to look through it so I have some background on your medical history."

Over the next half hour Poppy examined Autumn, went over her blood work and talked to her about upcoming tests.

A high-risk pregnancy. Chromosomal tests. Gestational diabetes test. A geriatric pregnancy. That one had caused her jaw to drop. She wasn't ancient by any stretch of the imagination, yet it seemed as if carrying a child at thirty-nine came with a lot of caution. Autumn swallowed past her nervousness.

"So, how are you feeling? You seem a bit overwhelmed," Poppy noted.

Autumn let out a sigh. So far she hadn't been able to confide in anyone about her pregnancy fears. She'd tried to project an air of confidence. It was nice to be able to confide in her doctor. "There are so many things to consider. I can't help but worry that my age is going to complicate this pregnancy. It's a bit overwhelming."

"Don't worry, Autumn. You're in great health. Any pregnancy over thirty-five is classified this way. There's no reason to think you won't carry this baby to term."

"Even though I was once told I would never be able to conceive?" Autumn asked, blinking away tears. Her endometriosis had been weighing on her mind. Would it affect her pregnancy or delivery?

Poppy's eyes widened. "Well, thankfully that isn't the case. It seems clear that the diagnosis was based on your endometriosis, which you've treated with surgery. That allowed you to get pregnant, which I'm guessing was a dream come true."

Autumn nodded. The condition had plagued her ever since her early twenties. Pain had been a part of her daily life for years. "Surgery was suggested by my doctor due to all the agony I was in. We never really talked about it reversing infertility." Due to her husband's lack of interest in having children, Autumn hadn't considered trying to get pregnant.

Dr. Poppy pointed at Autumn's abdomen. "Well, it did," she said. "You're really blessed. Some women struggle to conceive after thirty-five."

She mustered a smile even as her gut twisted. Autumn was over the moon about carrying this baby, but her whole life had been altered by that devastating news all those years ago. Her decision to end things with Judah had been a direct result of her infertility diagnosis. She had lost the love of her life and mourned the fact that she would never be a mother.

"There's no better way to convince you that the baby is fine than to let you see your little one with your own eyes," Poppy said with a smile. She instructed Autumn to sit back and lift up her shirt. "This might feel a little bit cold, but it'll be worth it," she said as she placed gel on her stomach and moved the probe in a circular motion.

Suddenly, Autumn could hear the sounds of a heartbeat and a small shape appeared on the screen that resembled a precious baby. Autumn let out a little cry as Poppy pointed out the head and spine.

"So, from what I see, your baby is doing beautifully." Poppy peered closely at the monitor. "I'm not able to determine gender due to the baby moving around so much, but maybe next time."

A tear slid down her face. "It's okay, Poppy. This appointment has been so reassuring. As long as I know everything is going smoothly,

I can wait to find out. It will be a nice surprise."

Poppy grinned. "That's what I'm here for, Autumn. To help you through the rest of your pregnancy," she said, reaching out and squeezing Autumn's hand. "I'd like to see you again in four weeks. If anything arises, don't hesitate to reach out."

"I will," Autumn promised. She would do whatever was required to bring a healthy child into the world. God had given her a chance at motherhood just when she had believed that door was firmly shut.

Autumn felt as if she was floating on air as she left the doctor's office with a photo of her baby in hand. She couldn't stop gazing at the black-and-white image. And even though she was still a little scared of the risks related to her pregnancy, a fragile hope was blossoming inside of her.

The day after Judah rescued Autumn by the pier, he didn't waste any time heading over to Northern Lights restaurant once he finished work. They'd ended the day early due to inclement weather. Judah wasn't ever going to take chances with the crew or his vessel. He'd been a commercial fisherman long enough to know the hazards of Alaskan waters. It was achingly beautiful, yet deadly at times.

Sean hadn't picked up his calls last night which was unusual for his friend. Some instinct told him Sean was feeling guilty about not warning him that Autumn had returned to Serenity Peak. His friendship with Sean spanned decades at this point. They had become instant friends in the sandbox in nursery school. They'd remained close even after Judah and Autumn's breakup. Sean had supported him like no other after the loss of Mary and Zane. He was more like a brother than Judah's own actual flesh and blood.

Judah stood outside the restaurant for a moment, admiring the gray façade with the white shutters. Northern Lights sat atop a cliff overlooking Kachemak Bay with the Serenity Mountains serving as a magnificent backdrop. The view always managed to take his breath away.

Although he tended to avoid the popular establishment, it was the only surefire way to track Sean down. Judah was a silent partner in the restaurant, having joined forces with Sean when he opened it fourteen years ago. Judah had stepped away to focus on the commercial fishing industry, which was a much better fit for him than dealing with the public. He knew he was at his best out on the water where he could seek out adventures and not have to deal with people. Thankfully, Sean had understood and they'd worked out a perfect arrangement, which included Judah providing fish for the restaurant and stepping in from time to time.

The moment he walked through the doors of Northern Lights, Judah breathed in the aroma of freshly grilled fish and roasted vegetables as well as rosemary fries and steak. The variety of scents made his stomach grumble with appreciation. But entering the eatery felt like being center stage. Small Alaskan towns like Serenity Peak didn't allow for many strangers. A quick glance around confirmed the fact that all of the diners were town residents he'd known for most of his life. Judah nodded to several who greeted him as he made his way to the back rooms. There were others he looked straight past. He would never forgive them for the nasty gossip they'd spread about his wife after the car wreck.

"Hey, Judah! You're a sight for sore eyes." The gravelly voice washed over him like a cozy blanket. Wally Hines, Autumn and Sean's dad, had a distinguished appearance with a head full of gray hair, twinkling eyes and a pair of wire-rimmed glasses. The older man had always been a huge influence in Judah's life.

Judah leaned in for a tight hug. "Hi, Wally. Looking good there," he said as the embrace ended. "You've lost some weight, I see." Wally was always looking to lose some pounds around his midsection, and it appeared he'd succeeded.

"Ten pounds. Thanks for noticing. I've missed you, son," Wally said with a grin. "If you're looking for Sean he's in the back with his head buried in the books." He let out a warm chuckle. "He'll be happy to see you."

As soon as he pushed past the swinging doors, Judah spotted Sean Hines through his open office door. Sean was standing at his desk looking through a pile of paperwork. Sean had the physique of a linebacker. He'd played for a minor league football team before blowing out his knee and leaving those aspirations behind. Everyone in Serenity Peak loved Sean. Judah had always believed that the success of Northern Lights was tied up in Sean's popularity rather than the amazing cuisine.

He stood in the doorway with his arms folded across his chest. "Hey there, Sean. You're a hard man to reach."

His best friend swung his head up and grinned at him. "Judah. Sorry about not returning your calls. I've been up to my ears in delivery issues and illnesses amongst the staff. We've had to scramble to get replacements." Sean riffled through some papers on his desk then looked back at Judah. "What's up? I'm surprised to see you here."

"Don't start with that," Judah protested. "I work long hours out on the water. I promise I'm not avoiding you."

"It's not me I'm worried about," Sean said with a shake of his head. "It's the rest of the town."

Fair point. Judah didn't even bother to challenge Sean's comment. He had spoken nothing but the truth. Most people in town weren't a priority for him. Not after what they'd said.

"So why didn't you tell me that Autumn was coming home?" Judah asked. "I was pretty shocked to see her at the pier." Judah didn't mention that he'd taken her to his house to get warm. He would let Autumn disclose that detail to Sean if she so desired. It wasn't as if anything had happened, but it still felt like information he should keep quiet about.

Sean sank down into a chair. Light brown eyes locked with his own. "I told you a long time ago that I didn't want to get in the middle of anything between you and Autumn. I love you both too much to get involved."

Judah sat on the corner of the desk. "I'm not asking that of you. I just didn't like being caught off guard." Especially by his first love. Judah ran a hand over his face. He didn't have to add that Autumn had blindsided him once before by calling it quits on their relationship. Try as he might to stuff the memory down, it still stung.

"I get it, Judah. And I'm sorry. To be honest, it felt awkward telling you that Autumn was pregnant and coming home to raise her baby here," Sean explained, quirking his mouth. "Honestly, it was a surprise to all of us. A happy one though."

"Babies are always a blessing," Judah said. "I'll never forget the day Zane was born." At nine pounds seven ounces, Zane had come into the world during a brutal snowstorm.

Sean nodded. "Me neither. I was honored to be his godfather. I miss him too, Judah. More than you know."

Sean and Zane had been particularly close. His best friend had taught his son how to throw a football and how to make collard greens, pot roast and quiche Lorraine. Sean had been Zane's honorary uncle.

"I know you do," Judah said. "And if I've never told you, I'm grateful for your friendship. Things could have gotten awkward between us after Autumn and I broke up but you never wavered." It was hard for Judah to tap into his emotions, but Sean needed to hear this. It was way overdue.

"Are you kidding me? There's nothing that could ever break up the dynamic duo." Judah could see Sean was fighting back tears. He was a big old softie. "That would be like Batman without Robin."

"Ain't that the truth," Judah said with a grin.

Sean leaned across the table and leaned on his forearms. "How about we grab some lunch? We can sit at our old table."

Judah made a face. "Sounds good, but I don't want to—"

"Don't even say it," Sean said, slicing his hand through the air. "You keep telling me that you want to move forward, but you're still stuck. I know you carry a lot of anger in your heart, Judah, and I don't blame you. The rumors about Mary being on pills when she crashed the car were hideous. Vicious. But you can't take it out on the entire town. It's not healthy."

Judah held up his hands in defeat. "Okay. If it means you'll can the lecture, let's go eat." At this point he knew it was better to give in than to protest. Plus, he was trying to change. Eating lunch in the dining area wouldn't kill him.

Sean stood up and cuffed his hand around the back of Judah's neck. "Come on. Let's do this!" Within minutes they were seated at their old table with a magnificent view of the mountains and the sparkling waters of the bay.

"Hey, boys. What can I get for you?" The familiar honeyed voice caused him to swing his head up in surprise. Autumn, wearing a Northern Lights T-shirt, stood by their table, with a small pad in her hand. The smile etched on her face caused his stomach to painfully twist.

Judah looked over at Sean and raised an eyebrow. Yet another thing Sean hadn't thought to mention. Autumn was waitressing at Northern Lights! A sheepish expression crept on to his friend's face. Sean burrowed his head in a menu he knew by memory.

"You're working here?" Judah asked as his gaze turned back to Autumn.

"I'm just filling in as a favor to Sean," Autumn said, looking over at her brother. "Like old times."

"I thought you'd be writing," Judah said. He'd gotten the impression being a writer was her focus for employment in Serenity Peak.

"She's actually on assignment for the *Alaska Tribune* focusing on local stories," Sean chimed in. Pride rang out in his voice. "Autumn is their newest hire."

"Wow. That's big time," Judah said. "The *Tribune* is one of the largest news outlets in the state."

Autumn sent Sean a loaded look then shifted uncomfortably from one foot to the other. "Yes, it's a great job. I'm happy to work a few hours here and there, as long as it doesn't interfere with my main gig." She let out a chuckle. "It means big bro now owes me a huge favor."

Sean chuckled. "As long as it doesn't involve changing dirty diapers I'm okay with that."

Judah laughed along with them. The idea

of Sean dealing with a dirty diaper wasn't something he could picture. Sean was married to a wonderful woman named Helene. They had three kids ranging in age from five to thirteen. As Sean often liked to say, he was done changing diapers. Been there, done that. Judah knew his friend was completely serious.

Autumn quickly took their order and promised to return with two waters. She'd seemed slightly on edge. Something was up with her. Judah knew her well enough to know when she was unsettled. The look she'd given Sean had hidden meaning. She'd been a nervous wreck with trembling hands. Judah couldn't help but wonder if it had something to do with the baby she was carrying. It was none of his business, especially since they had been out of each other's lives for more than a decade, but he prayed that she delivered a healthy baby. If not, Autumn would be shattered.

Autumn hated having a guilty conscience. Waiting on Judah and Sean was nerve-racking. Her brother had shaken her by mentioning her employment with the *Tribune* in front of Judah. What would she have said if Judah had asked her what stories she was working on? She wasn't prone to lying, but telling him the truth might prove to be awkward. Sean had previously told her that Judah was aware of fraud allegations being tied to the local fishing community. But did he have any idea that he and his operation might be under the microscope? Never in a million years could she imagine Judah underreporting his fishing hauls, mislabeling fish or catching fish in unauthorized areas. He was honest to a fault.

Judah was an honorable man. Or at least he had been back in the day. People didn't change who they were at their core.

Once Sean finished lunch with Judah and headed back to his office, Autumn followed behind her brother. She needed to warn him against telling Judah about her assignment from the *Tribune*. If necessary, Autumn would tell him herself.

Autumn entered Sean's office with purposeful strides. She felt like a kid who'd gotten their hand caught in the cookie jar. She'd only arrived in Serenity Peak a few days ago and she was already tiptoeing around.

"What's wrong?" Sean asked, knitting his brows together. "You look upset."

She twisted her mouth. "You shouldn't have mentioned my working for the *Tribune* in front of Judah," Autumn said. "I'm writing a piece on the local commercial fishing industry, Sean. Allegations of underreporting catch and falsifying records are serious. Judah's operation is one of the most profitable in this area. It stands to reason that he might be under scrutiny."

"So what? Are you saying that Judah is involved in something illegal?" Sean asked in a raised tone.

"I'm not saying anything of the sort." She let out a frustrated sound. "But it's my job to be as objective as I can in my reporting and follow where the story leads me." She didn't want to say even if it led straight to Judah.

A sound in the doorway caused Autumn to turn in that direction. Judah was standing there looking confused. "I came back to get my keys," he said, jerking his chin in the direction of Sean's desk where the keys sat. "Autumn. Please tell me you're not writing a hit piece about the local fishing industry."

"Judah. I can explain," she said, swallowing past the lump in her throat.

Sean threw up his hands and said, "This is between the two of you. Just keep it down to a dull roar." With a shake of his head, Sean left his office, closing the door behind him with a little bang.